W9-BID-881

BASED ON A NATIVE AMERICAN FOLKTALE

TURTLE'S BIG RACE

Written by Alice Leonhardt
Illustrated by Don Tate

STECK-VAUGHN
ELEMENTARY · SECONDARY · ADULT · LIBRARY

® A Harcourt Classroom Education Company

www.steck-vaughn.com

All winter Turtle slept at the bottom of his pond.

He dreamed about sunning himself on his logs.

He dreamed about playing on his rocks.

Now spring was here.

Turtle swam to the top of the water.

He popped out his head and looked around.

"What has happened to my pond?" Turtle cried.

The water was too deep!

It covered his favorite logs and rocks.

Bang! Boom! Crash!

Turtle turned to see what made all the noise.

An animal was cutting down Turtle's trees!

Turtle swam through the water.
He climbed out of the pond.
"Who are you?" Turtle asked the furry animal.
"And what are you doing to **my** pond?"

"I am Beaver," the furry animal said.
"And I am building a dam in **my** pond."

"Well, Beaver, I want you to stop!" Turtle said.
Beaver laughed at Turtle and kept on chewing.
Turtle was so mad that he snapped his jaws.
How could he get rid of that pesky Beaver?
"Let's have a contest!" Turtle told Beaver.
"Only the winner will get to live at the pond."

"Let's have a tail whacking contest," Beaver said.

Turtle looked at Beaver's long, wide tail.
Then Turtle looked at his own short, skinny tail.
He would never win a tail whacking contest.
"No, let's race across the pond," Turtle said.
His webbed feet just might help him win.

Beaver and Turtle lined up on the shore.
They dove into the water and swam hard.
Beaver's wide tail helped him swim fast.
Soon Beaver was ahead of Turtle!
Turtle had to come up with a plan.
He decided that Beaver could help him win.

Turtle grabbed Beaver's fat tail with his jaws.
"Let go!" Beaver yelled.
Beaver smacked his tail hard on the water.

Turtle flew right over Beaver's head.
Turtle landed on the shore in front of Beaver.
"I am the winner!" Turtle shouted.

"Now you must leave **my** pond," Turtle told Beaver.

"But I helped you win the race," Beaver said sadly.

Turtle knew that Beaver was right.
"Then let's share the pond," Turtle said.
"We'll work together to make it the best pond ever!"